Pinocchio

Once upon a time, in a country far away, there lived a carpenter
called Geppetto. He had a kind heart and desperately wanted a child.
One day in his workshop, he found a small piece of wood
and decided to carve a little puppet.

When he had carved the wood and was just putting the final touches on the puppet's face, he heard someone speak. 'Ouch! That hurts!' The puppet began to talk and move. He was alive! Geppetto decided to name him Pinocchio.

Pinocchio was a very active puppet.
He liked to run and jump, and he filled the house with joy.
Sometimes he was a naughty boy.

One day, when he was really being particularly naughty,
Pinocchio heard a chirping. 'You shouldn't do that!
Your father will be upset!' He turned around and saw a wise, talking
cricket but instead of listening, he continued to misbehave.

Kindly Geppetto loved the puppet,
but he was worried about how mischievous Pinocchio was.
'I'm going to send you to school
where you can learn to behave properly.'
Geppetto sold his own jacket to buy Pinocchio's schoolbook.

But Pinocchio wasn't happy. 'I don't want to go to school!
I like to run around and chase butterflies!'
He took the book and set off on foot.

On the way to school, Pinocchio
came upon a marionette theatre.
Curious, he decided to sell his book to buy a ticket.
When the marionettes saw him, they began to shout,
'Run away, puppet! Run away!'

The puppet master didn't like all the commotion in his theatre.
He grabbed Pinocchio and started to throw him out.
But then he had a change of heart.
'You're not even good for kindling. I feel sorry for you.
Take these five gold coins and get out of here!'

Pinocchio ran away, but on the road he met
two strange characters: a cat and a fox.
'What lovely gold coins. Give them to us, puppet!
We'll plant them in the Field of Miracles.
A money tree will grow, and you'll be rich!'
Pinocchio was fooled by their promises,
and they stole his coins and tied him to a tree
so he couldn't chase them.

A young woman with blue hair approached Pinocchio.

'What beautiful hair!' Pinocchio exclaimed.
The young woman, the Blue Fairy, recited a spell and got him
out of the tree.'What were you doing up there?' she asked.

Pinocchio didn't want to admit the truth,
and each time he told a lie his nose grew.
'Pinocchio, behave yourself!' the Blue Fairy said.

Pinocchio knew he should tell the judge his story
and get his coins back, but instead he kept telling lies.
He was sent to prison!
Meanwhile, Geppetto was very worried about Pinocchio
and went looking for him all over town.
When Pinocchio didn't come home, Geppetto built
a rowboat and set out to sea to search for him.

He couldn't keep his promise, though.
He met a lazy boy with bad manners
who convinced him
to travel to the Land of Toys.

The Land of Toys was so much fun,
and Pinocchio played all day
and didn't have to work.
But then something strange
occurred. 'Hee-haw!'

What happened to
Pinocchio's ears?
And where did he get
that tail?

Pinocchio turned into
a donkey and was sold
to the circus.

While putting on a show,
he fell and hurt himself.
What would happen now?

Pinocchio was no longer of any use to the circus,
so he was thrown into the sea.
Luckily, the Blue Fairy sent some fish to free him
from his donkey harness and turn him back into a puppet.
Pinocchio tried to swim to the surface,
but something scared him! A whale!

The puppet swam as fast as he could,
but he couldn't escape the whale.
The whale ate Pinocchio and he went right into its stomach.
But who else was there?

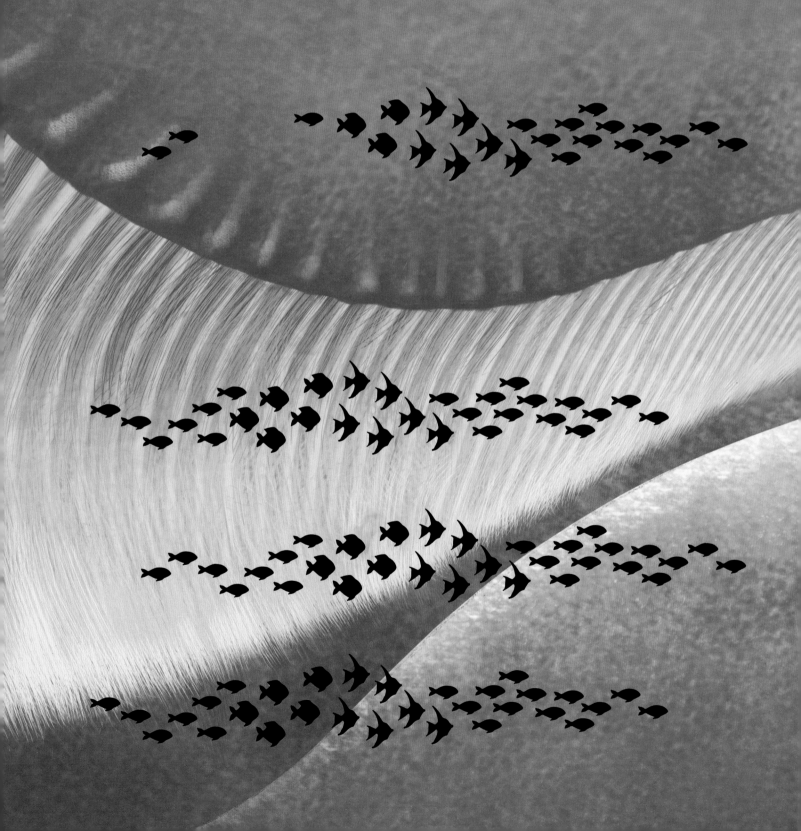

Pinocchio had found his father, Geppetto,
and when night fell and the whale was sleeping
with its mouth hanging open,
the two of them escaped.

Pinocchio and Geppetto went home,
tired from their adventures.
Pinocchio had changed and he began to study hard
and help his father around the house.

When the Blue Fairy saw that Pinocchio had finally learnt
his lesson, she rewarded him by turning Geppetto's hut into a
beautiful house, gave them both new clothes and, best of all,
she turned Pinocchio into a real boy!